Donated
by the
FRIENDS
of
Pickens Library

CARL HELPS ON THE FARM

by Avis Rector

For Grandpa George, Carl, Scott and Andy

ISBN #
0-89716-572-1
Library of Congress #
95-069-874

Designer: Robert Dietz
Editor: Elizabeth Lake
Photography & Illustration: Avis Rector

First Printing
10 9 8 7 6 5 4 3 2 1

Peanut Butter Publishing
226 2nd Avenue West
Seattle, WA 98119

Printed in Korea

It was spring at the farm.

The lawn, the fields, the new leaves on the trees were all green. Dew on the grass sparkled in the sunshine. Baby birds chirped from their nests in the trees. Baby calves played chase in the pasture.

Carl had come to the farm to visit his Grandma and Grandpa. He was sitting at the table eating blueberries and cereal. "Look, Grandma, there's a little hummingbird!"

Grandma looked out the window. She saw a pretty humming-bird drinking sweet nectar from the pink and purple fuchsia.

Grandma sat down at the table. "There's lots of work to be done today. The spring rain and bright sunshine made everything look pretty and green but the weeds grew too. I wonder who will help me weed the flower beds?"

"I will help you, Grandma," offered Carl.

"We must wear our boots," said Grandma. "I have new yellow boots."

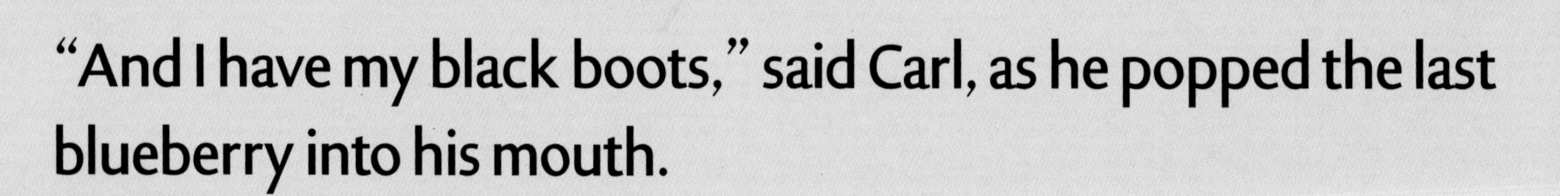

"And I have my black boots," said Carl, as he popped the last blueberry into his mouth.

Carl and Grandma went to the shed. They brought out the garden tools.

"What are these called?" asked Carl.

"These are garden tools ... implements," Grandma answered. "This is a trowel," she explained as she held it up in the air.

"I like to call it . . . implement," said Carl.

They took all the implements out by the big rock garden. They put the weeds in the brown bucket, taking time to admire the bright red tulips.

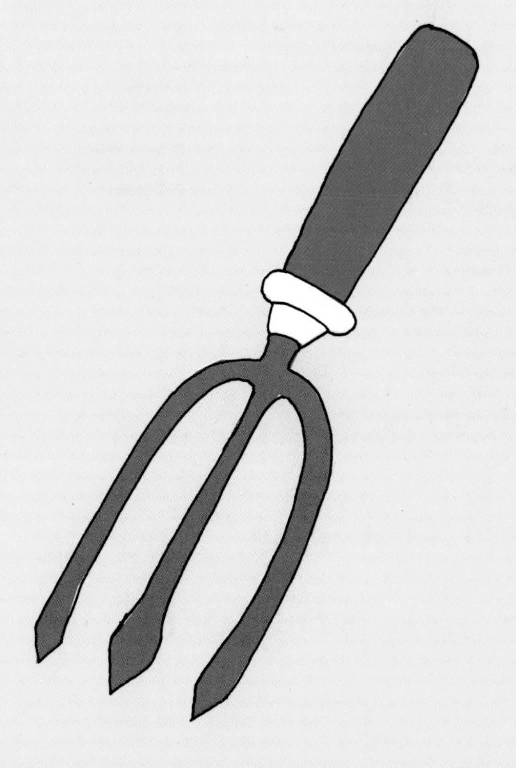

Grandma gave Carl a boost so he could sit on a big rock.

"It feels warm, Grandma. Grandma, look! Bees! Get me down!" shouted Carl.

"You're okay," Grandma assured him. "Bees like the nectar in the crabapple blossoms. They won't hurt you."

"I see Grandpa," said Carl. "Grandpa, we're out here! Look at me on this big rock!"

"Carl, I need help at the barn. Will you help me?" asked Grandpa.

"I will help you, Grandpa," Carl said, sliding down off the big rock.

As they walked through the green pasture, they stopped to look at some cows and their calves. Carl stroked the cow's hair. It felt smooth and warm.

“The bull needs water,” said Grandpa. “His water tank is empty.”

“I can give him water. He needs lots of water because he’s thirsty,” Carl said as he held the hose to fill the tank. He was careful not to spill the water. He was a good helper.

"The bull needs hay, too," said Grandpa.

"I'll get it, Grandpa. I'll get some hay!" said Carl as he ran into the barn.

Grandpa used his big knife to cut the orange string on the bale of hay. "Can you carry this section?" he asked.

"Okay. Sure!" said Carl. "This is not too much for me. I'm big."

"That was good help," said Grandpa. "Now I have a surprise for you."

"What is it?" asked Carl.

"Come with me and you'll see," Grandpa said.

Carl took Grandpa's hand and skipped along beside him. "I like surprises. I wonder what it is. Will you tell me?"

Grandpa laughed. "Do you remember Sunshine? She has the surprise."

As they went through the gate into another pasture Carl looked around. “Grandpa, look! Sunshine has a baby!”

“That’s the surprise,” said Grandpa. “A new calf having its first breakfast.”

“Can I pet it?” asked Carl.

“We’ll come back later,” said Grandpa, “after it’s finished nursing.”

“Let’s go tell Grandma,” said Carl, “she likes surprises, too.”

Grandma did like the surprise, but she had something else on her mind. “It’s time to plant the garden and I need help. Who will help me?”

“I will help you,” said Grandpa. “I’ll till the garden.”

“I will help you too, Grandma!” said Carl.

They all worked in the garden. Grandma said the soil was so good.

“What is soil?” asked Carl.

“This is nice soft soil,” explained grandma, as she let the soil sift through her fingers. “We will plant the seeds in the warm soil.”

“I call it dirt,” said Carl.

“I call it dirt when it gets on your face,” laughed Grandma, “but I call it soil when it’s in the garden.”

“I like to dig in the soil,” replied Carl, thoughtfully.

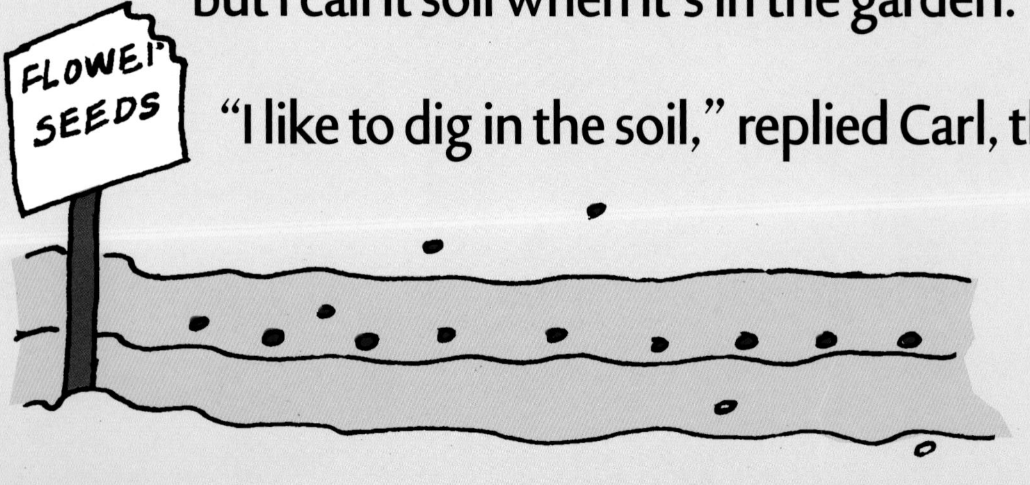

After grandpa tilled the soil, Grandma and Carl worked in their gardens. Grandma planted potatoes, spinach, peas and lettuce. Carl planted beets, radishes and flowers.

"Thank you for helping in the garden, Carl," Grandma said.

"You are a good helper."

They found Grandpa working by the barn.

"Look!" said Grandpa. "Here's a caterpillar for you, Carl."

Carl took the caterpillar. It tickled as it crawled up his arm.

"It won't hurt me," he said, "I want to keep it."

He carried it to the house in his hand.

Grandma brought out a big jar.

They put leaves from the apple tree into the jar.

The caterpillar crawled on the leaves.

"I need help," said Grandma, as she covered the top of the jar with plastic wrap.

"I will help you," said Carl.

He put the rubber band over the plastic to tightly hold it on the jar. He poked holes in the plastic so the caterpillar would have air.

"Now your caterpillar will stay in the jar and you can watch him eat his snack," explained Grandma.

"I'm hungry, too," said Carl.

So Carl and his caterpillar ate their snacks.

"Is there anyone here who would like to help mow the lawn?" asked Grandpa.

"Me!" exclaimed Carl. "I would like to help you."

Carl helped Grandpa steer the lawn mower. He was careful not to hurt the flowers.

He was a good helper.

While Grandpa sharpened the lawn mower, Carl rode his tractor. Suddenly he stopped. "The power on my tractor is broken, but I can fix it."

Grandpa gave him a screwdriver to fix his tractor.

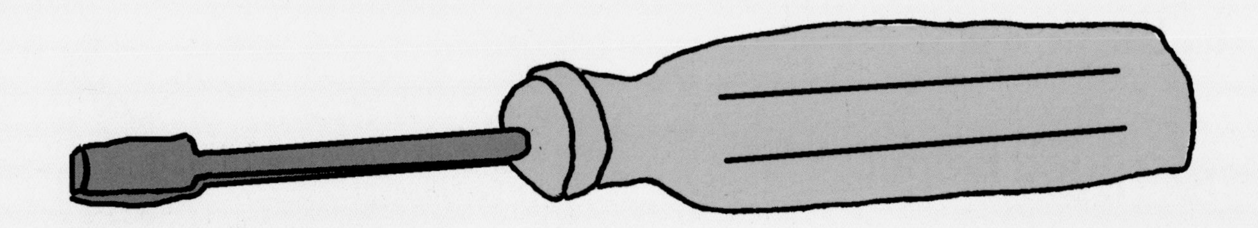

Grandma wanted to wash the screen door, but she was having trouble taking out the screws.

“I can do it, Grandma!” Carl said, excitedly, “I can help you!”

He used his screwdriver to take out all the screws. After the screen had been cleaned, Carl put the screws back in their holes.

He had done a good job. He was a very good helper.

Every day at the farm was a busy day.

Carl helped move the cows from one pasture to another.

"I'm not afraid Grandpa, I chase the cows with my big stick."

He watered his garden so the little seeds would grow.

He used his implements to dig in the nice, warm soil.

It was fun to help Grandpa drive the tractor.

Carl held on tight to the steering wheel.

He turned to the left and to
the right.

He was a good helper.

He washed Grandma's yellow boots and his black boots.

His clothes got all wet.

"That's okay, Grandma, I can put on my other pants."

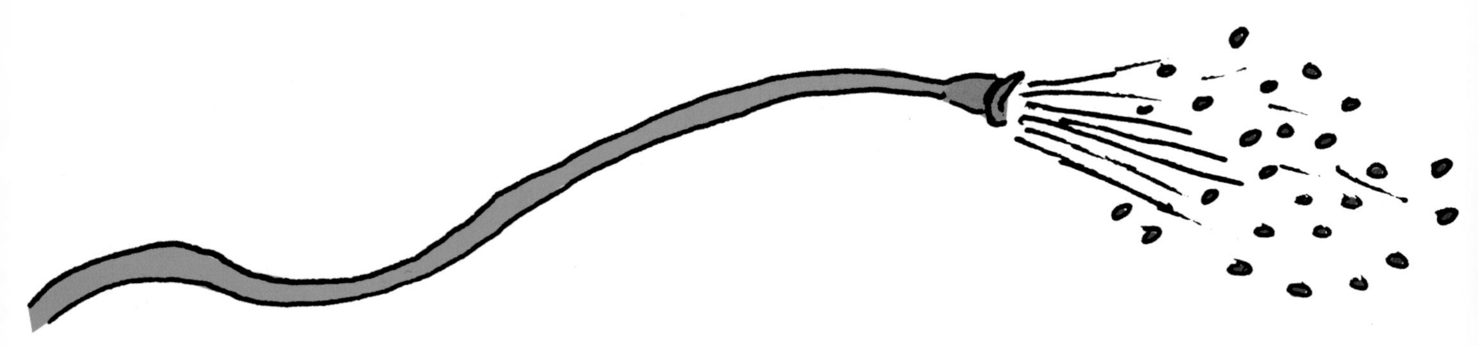

Carl sent pictures and letters to his mom, dad and brother, Scott.

He sent pictures and a letter to his cousin, Andy.

He told them how he had fun helping on the farm.

Dear Scott,
I put seeds in the soil.

Love,
CARL